Contents

Chapter 1

It was Christmas at Mrs Crabs' house. The tree was flashing away like it was advertising striptease. There were little coloured lightbulbs twinkling all round the windows and mirrors. On the wall outside there was a big sign going on and off, saying, *Merry Christmas, Merry Christmas* in red, green and gold.

Mrs Crabs loved that sort of thing. She had decorations looping backwards and forwards all over the room. There was plastic holly on the front door and enough mistletoe to snog Manchester. Balloons hung in every corner and there was a bloody great log fire blazing away in the sitting room, even though everyone was far too hot. Christmas Day at her house had been a fixture for years, ever since she topped Harry Dobson and took over gangland.

You can call me Mikey. Christmas with Mrs C scared me, it was out of my class. I'd never have been invited if I wasn't going out with Maggie Milligan.

Maggie was out of my class too. She was smart, beautiful and deadly. I'd have dropped her years ago if I'd known what was good for me. But once you've had a taste of a girl like that … well, you don't just chuck her away. And anyway, it was a good career move. Everyone knows that the Milligan family are on the way up, and the Crabs are on the way down.

Yeah, I know. It sounds like a quick way to get killed. OK. Call me soft. I'd fallen in love.

We got there about ten o'clock and first thing, even before we opened the presents, Mrs Crabs announced that Joey Milligan had it coming. She had her sons Nick and Greg tie him up by his feet in the middle of the sitting room with his hands tied behind his back. Then she beat the shit out of him with her walking stick.

At first I thought it was going to be a party game. Charlie and Brenda Milligan, his mum and dad, stood there arm in arm watching like a pair of old penguins. That wasn't like Charlie when his boy was in trouble.

When Mrs Crabs had newspaper put down on the carpet under him, I knew it was serious. The thing that really got me was she got his mam to help. Her husband Eddie was doing a perfectly good job spreading out old copies of the *Daily Mail* under Joey. But Mrs Crabs nodded at Brenda.

"You too, Brenda," she said. It was an order.

Brenda shuddered, but Charlie said, "You better had, Bren," and so she got down on her knees to help.

I mean, that was not nice. I thought, what the fuck is going on? I opened my mouth, but there was Greg and Nick standing right next to me so I shut up quick.

She started off on his ribs and then went down across his face. He didn't have much face left by the time she set Nick and Greg on him. After he stopped making any noise at all, she had him cut down and carted away upstairs. Eddie cleaned up the newspaper while the rest of us stood about drinking cocktails as if nothing had happened.

What was going on? Charlie and Brenda Milligan were taking a glass of champagne from Greg Crabs, who'd just murdered their boy. I couldn't understand it. Yesterday they were not far off pushing the Crabs off their perch. Now here they were standing about like prats while their only boy got turned into dog meat.

Eddie found some spots of blood on the little silver balls on the Christmas tree and started cleaning them up with his hanky. I watched him wiping away and tutting to himself and I thought, you little shit. She does the business with her stick and he stands round polishing her balls for her. Mrs Crabs was a psycho, but he was just dirt. He tried to make out he was the boss but no one was fooled. If it wasn't for her, no one would even look at him.

"Keep your balls clean, Mr Crabs," I told him with a friendly nod. He looked at me like he wanted mine on a plate.

Me and my big mouth. I shouldn't have said that. The way things were going, he was likely to get them.

The Old Bag made us wait while she checked up on the decorations. She made Eddie re-hang a streamer she'd knocked down with her stick, and got one of the girls to put Vanish on the carpet where the blood had soaked through. Then she sat herself down on the arm of a chair. Eddie clapped his hands twice to attract attention. If it'd been me I'd have died of shame, but he seemed to like it.

"Thank you, Eddie," said Mrs Crabs, and she smiled round the room. She looked like a little grey rabbit wearing glasses. "Our Joey's been grassing us up," she said.

There was dead silence. Joey, a grass? Impossible! But we all knew she must have the goods on him for Charlie and Brenda to stand there and watch it.

She wagged her stick in Charlie's face. "I don't mind your family making a bid for it, Charlie," she said, "but your boy used the filth to do it. If I ever get a whiff that you and Brenda and most of all your Maggie are using the same tricks, you'll get the same, Christmas or not." She wrinkled up her nose as if there was a nasty smell. "And that goes for anyone else who gets involved. I can't help noticing that Maggie isn't with us today," she added. And she gave me a long, dirty look.

I could have wet myself just standing there. "She said she'd be here, I thought she'd be here," I said.

I could see Greg and Nick looking at me, too, and I thought, *Oh, shit*. Everyone had been certain that the Milligans were on the Way Up and the Crabs were on the Way Down. Now ... Happy Christmas! Joey Milligan was dog meat, Maggie hadn't turned up, and Charlie and Brenda were standing there trying to look as if their own kids had nothing to do with them.

I never fell out of love so fast in all my life.

"You can open your presents, now," said Mrs Crabs.

Chapter 2

After the turkey we were all sent out to walk round the garden a few times.

"Work it down, boys. Make room for Christmas pud," said Mrs Crabs cheerily, holding the door open for us.

We all trooped out and started going slowly round under the apple trees, sticking carefully to the little stone path. Mrs Crabs doesn't like the grass getting trod on in winter. The stupid path's only about a foot wide. It was a laugh, watching them big blokes carefully putting one foot in front of the other so they didn't walk on the grass.

Or it would have been a laugh if I hadn't been one of them.

I slid over towards poor old Charlie and Brenda. I felt for them. No one had been speaking to them all morning and anyhow, it'd be pretty shit if I just dumped them both without so much as a backward glance, wouldn't it? I wasn't planning on seeing anything of them or Maggie after today, but I could at least say goodbye.

I said, "What the fuck's going on, then?"

Charlie looked at me like his tongue was going to turn into cat shit in his mouth and he said, "It's true, Mikey. The stupid sod was making deals with the filth."

"Not Joey! I can't believe it."

"She's got a tape of him with the filth. Here, you can have a listen yourself.

Everyone else will, soon enough." He produced a tape from his pocket and handed it over, shaking his head. "I couldn't believe it. Me own flesh and blood."

Brenda Milligan dabbed her nostrils with a piece of manky tissue. "He's let us all down, Mikey."

"I can't believe it. Joey and the filth!" Charlie shook his head again and his eyes filled up with tears.

Joey knew the rules. He brought it on himself ... and on Brenda and Charlie. Fancy doing that to your own family! And he'd brought it on me and Maggie, too. You'd have to be barmy to go with her after tonight. It was all over between us, and it was Joey's fault.

"But making you and his mam watch ... that was wrong, Charlie. She shouldn't of done that no matter what he did."

We all looked over at the house. *Once in Royal David's City* was leaking out of the half-open door. There was Mrs Crabs in the kitchen window with Greg and Nick, drinking champagne and laughing their heads off. The bloody Old Bag. She was right back in charge. Joey had handed it to her on a plate. I tell you, I'd have liked to have a go with that stick on him myself. He'd shafted the lot of us, him and his big mouth.

Brenda Milligan lifted the tissue off her big red nose long enough to hiss, "The fucking little shite always wanted to go too fast. Another couple of months and we'd have had her flat on the carpet," she began. But she had to shut up quick because a couple of the lads came pacing down the garden towards us.

"All right, boys?" I nodded, but they hardly gave me a glance. Let's face it, I was mixed up with the wrong lot. They walked past as if Charlie and Brenda were a hole in the ground. It was going to be a long time before any of the Milligans could hold their heads up in Manchester again.

When they'd gone past, Charlie said, "I don't mind about us, it's you young ones that I worry about. You too, Mikey. I know how much Maggie loves you. You're almost family now."

"You're all our Maggie's got now, Mikey," blubbed Brenda. "I know you'll do yer best by her, won't you son? That girl thinks the world of you, you know that, don't you?"

And you know what? My heart did a jump for joy. I felt as though someone had just hit me with a pick axe. She loved me! She'd never told me, but she loved me all the time. "I didn't know she felt like that," I croaked.

"Oh, Mikey, the love that girl has for you!

She's always talking about you, isn't she Charlie?"

Charlie nodded. "She's got it bad for you, Mikey," he said. "She adores you."

I wiped my eyes on the back of my hand and hoped none of the Crabs could see me doing it. I was thinking of all the times I wanted to tell her how much I loved her and never did because I was sure she didn't love me back ... and she did, she did love me, the whole time.

"Where is she today, then?" I asked.

"I don't know. We thought she'd be coming with you." Charlie gave Brenda a look, and then he said, "I won't hide it from you, Mikey. The Old Bag reckons that Maggie was in on it with Joey."

Brenda groaned. Charlie patted her

hand. "Don't worry, Bren. I don't believe a word of it, she's just turning the heat on," he said.

"Well, where's our Maggie today, then?" hissed Brenda angrily. "If she's turned grass, she'll get hers just like Joey has. I'll string her up meself. But it breaks me heart to say it, son, it breaks me heart," she said.

Poor old Charlie just burst into tears as he stood there.

"Not Maggie, she never would," he gurgled. He pointed his finger at me and said, "Not our Maggie." They both looked utterly destroyed.

Eddie Crabs came out of the back door and yelled, "Come and get it! Pud's ready! Come and get it!"

Charlie wiped his eyes on the back of his

hand. Brenda buried her nose in a tissue. We wandered up the little path and back indoors for the Christmas pud.

I felt sick. I didn't know what to do. I sat there poking my pudding around my plate and trying to think. So many questions!

One thing I did understand, though. All this explained why I had a card from Maggie in my back pocket telling me to meet her tomorrow night at Brady's Bar. Well, I wasn't going. I'd made up my mind. I may have a soft heart, but I'm not stupid.

Chapter 3

Brady's Bar is one of those Irish places with crap limericks up on the walls and a shamrock stamped on top of your Guinness. No one I know ever goes there any more. The place is full of office workers and off-duty filth.

OK, OK ... I shouldn't have gone. I know that. But Maggie was my girlfriend. She loved me. Of course, this was going to be the last time we'd be able to meet. She'd understand that. It was impossible for us to keep on seeing each other after what had happened, but I had to say goodbye, didn't I?

I was shitting myself as I went in the door. What if it was a set-up? Mrs Crabs and her boys would just love to get their hands on Maggie ... and me with her, if it came to that.

I crept in, got a pint, sat down and waited to see if it was Maggie, or Greg and Nick who'd turn up. It didn't take long. Down came the hand on the shoulder. I turned round to see this big black bloke dressed in an anorak about two sizes too big, looking down at me. He had two huge silver rings in his nose, one on each side. They looked like two great, big, weird bogeys.

"Maggie sent me," he said.

I tried to look confused. I had no idea whose side he was on. "Maggie who?" I said.

He bent down to me and hissed, "Maggie fucking Thatcher, who else? Listen, mate, I don't have time to play silly buggers. If you wanna see your girlfriend, get outside quick."

"How do I know you're who you say you are?" I asked, but he just shrugged. That was my problem.

I said, "Where outside?"

"Waterstone's."

"Water-what?"

"Bookshop. Deansgate, opposite Kendals. She'll be in the Art department on the first floor. Got it?"

I nodded. He turned round and walked off. I waited a few minutes and then followed on. I saw him again a few minutes later in the bookshop, lurking about outside the Art department. It looked like Maggie had found herself a minder.

There she was all right, standing in front of the shelves flicking through a book. I was relieved I wasn't going to get done over, but I was scared silly for Maggie. She looked so helpless and sweet standing there, with her soft brown hair and her pretty pink face. She pushed her hair to one side and gave me a long, nervous look with her big wide apart eyes. I thought of Mrs Crabs' stick going bang-bang-bang against that face, and what Greg and Nick might get up to if they caught her. I felt sick with it already.

I walked over and looked at the book. It was black and white photos of people with long, miserable, wrinkled faces. She always had some odd tastes, Maggie.

I nodded at one of them and said, "He looks like how I feel."

She laughed at me and shook her head. "Oh, it's good to see you, Mikey." She put the book down on a table next to her and flung her arms around my neck and hugged me tight. I put my arms round her waist and buried my face in her neck. She smelled so good. She had her tits pushed up into my chest.

I kissed her neck and whispered, "I'm so sorry, babe. I'm so sorry."

She just squeezed me back and shook her head. She knew there was nothing I could have done about it. We stood there for maybe a minute or more, just holding one another, and me trying not to get turned on because, let's face it, it wasn't the time or the place.

The mood was broken when I spotted the big black guy with the nose rings watching us from behind a rack of magazines.

I put her down and stepped back. "Who's the minder, then?" I asked, nodding over to him.

"Oh, that's just Jeff. Dad sent him along to keep an eye on me."

"Right." I picked up a book and leafed through it. "So why the bookshop? What's wrong with a nice pub?" I asked.

"How many of Mrs Crabs' lot do you know who drink?" she asked.

"All of them."

"And how many of them read books?"

"Yeah, well. Point taken." I grinned. Like I said, she's smart, our Maggie. Always one step ahead.

I flicked through the pages of my book. "Joey and the filth, eh? Who'd have thought

it. I'd never have put him down as a grass."
I looked at her out of the corner of my eye.
"Sorry, Maggie, but he's really blown it for
everyone, you can't deny it."

She hung her head and shook her hair
over her face. She always does that when
she cries, to hide her tears. She said, "It's a
set-up, Mikey."

I shook my head. I knew she'd find it
hard to accept. But ...

"I've heard the tape, Maggie."

"It's a set-up," she repeated. "Do you
think Joey would waste his time with the
filth? He hated them as much as anyone,
you know that."

"I heard the tape, Maggie."

"Tapes can be faked. Look ..." She held
on to my arm. "Joey was getting too

powerful, that's why Mrs Crabs had him topped. She knew she couldn't do it straight off because he had too many people on his side. This way, everyone thinks he got what he deserved. And I'll tell you something else, Mikey. She's going to get me next. She's already telling people I've been grassing, same as Joey. Mikey, I'm scared she's going to have me hanging up there next. If Nick and Greg ever get their hands on me ..."

She hid her tears with her hair again, and I thought my heart was going to break.

"You've got to get out of town, Maggie. It's the only thing for it. Look, I'll help you, but you've got to go away."

She shook her head. "I'm not having people think our Joey was a grass. People have to know what the Old Bag's doing, Mikey. I'm not going anywhere until my family's been put in the clear."

"Are you off your head? Everyone's heard the tape. How can I help you if you won't let me?"

"OK." She wiped away her tears and looked up at me. She looked so brave, but I could have wept. She had to get away! "You've heard the bullshit from Mrs Crabs. Now you can hear the truth from me."

Maggie checked there was no one near before she took an envelope out of her bag and handed it to me. It was photos. First off was a black and white photo of a blonde bombshell. You know the sort ... fluffy blonde hair, pointy tits, little tight jumper tucked in her skirt. She was hanging onto the arm of a big bloke in a monkey suit.

"Pretty," I said.

"Mrs Crabs," said Maggie.

"What?" Now that was hard to take. It was difficult to imagine Mrs Crabs ever having been under fifty. I peered at the face in the photo. Was it really the same woman who beat a bloke to death with her walking stick yesterday? I tried to see past the years and through all that lipstick and face powder. Well, maybe. Same narrow jaw, same hard little eyes.

I said, "Maybe."

"It's her all right. Nineteen years old and already shagging and murdering her way up the ladder."

"Gangland gangbang, was it?"

"It was one at a time as far as I know. Not all of them lived to tell the tale."

I had a revolting picture in me mind of Mrs Crabs in bed with some bloke on top of her, hips pumping away while she ate off the top of his head. I said, "Who's the poor bastard she's got her claws on here, then? How long did he last?"

"A few years. He cleared off and opened a casino in London in the end. But the thing is, see, there was a kid. Yeah, a baby boy. Mrs Crabs isn't the one to be left holding the baby."

"So?"

"So she had him fostered. She kept in touch, though. Visited him every Sunday for years. And thirty years later ... hey presto ..."

She handed me another photo.

"Fucking hell! You're joking. Not Primo! You're not telling me Detective Sergeant Primo is Mrs Crabs' fucking love child?"

"You got it in one, Mikey."

I peered closely at the photo. Detective Sergeant Andy Primo, standing there smiling away like anything with little old Mrs Crabs holding onto his arm. Mother and son? Wow!

"Jesus," I said, "You're right. Look, they've got the same mean, crabby little eyes. Jesus, they've even got the same teeth! And look at that fucking horrible smile. God, who'd have dreamed that? Old Mrs Crabs has family in the force."

"Very handy."

"Yeah?"

"Ever wondered how come Primo worked his way up so fast when he's thick as shit? Ever wondered how come Mrs Crabs always manages to be one step ahead of the old filth? How come anyone who gets in her way ends up inside? And if they don't end up inside, some sort of evidence comes up that they've been grassing. What about the tape of Joey? Who's doing the interview?"

"Primo."

"And those other tapes that Mrs Crabs got her hands on last year. Who were all those other blokes grassing to?"

"Primo!"

"Who made the arrests the year before that, when that Asian gang were trying to take over her territory?"

"Fucking Primo! Jesus! So the Old Bag has been getting Primo to frame our blokes. He makes a lot of arrests and gets promotion. She gets rid of anyone who's in her way. But she's got you stitched up, hasn't she, Maggie? No one's going to believe you. There's nothing we can do to prove that Mrs Crabs and Primo are family."

"Oh, yes there is." Maggie smiled grimly. "She's got the whole family history written down. Scrap books, photos, the lot. Little baby Primo's christening mug. His first drawings. Everything. She can't bear to throw 'em away. She keeps 'em in a box under the boards in her bedroom. And you're going to nick it."

"Like fuck I am," I said.

Chapter 4

Stupidity runs in my family. There I was, creeping round Mrs Crabs' house at four o'clock in the afternoon with Maggie's minder, Jeff. *Merry Christmas* was still flashing on and off outside. The Christmas tree was still twinkling away, but the balloons had gone all wrinkly. The alarms were all out of action ... at least, the ones we knew about were. There were bound to be more. A woman in Mrs Crabs' position needed as many alarms as she could get.

We had to work fast.

I'd had the shakes all afternoon, but as soon as we got inside I began shuddering. I couldn't help it. We were mad! Then me legs packed in and I stopped dead two feet up the stairs in the hall.

Jeff was right behind me. He had his nose rings out for the job. He poked me in the back. "What's up?"

"I can't do it," I hissed.

"Don't be stupid."

"You don't fucking understand. The Old Bag'll do anything to us if she catches us!"

"Don't think about it … and don't tell me about it, either."

"I'm too bloody scared, mate, I'm too scared. Me legs won't fucking work. There'll be alarms ringing all over town. They'll be here any minute!"

"Then bloody hurry up," snarled Jeff. He shoved his crowbar in me back and ran me up the stairs like he was pushing a kid on its way to bed. He was a big bloke, Jeff. Then he dashed into the back bedroom and seconds later I could hear him ripping up the carpet.

Well, I couldn't bottle out with him getting on with it, could I? I tiptoed along the landing to the main bedroom where Mrs C slept.

I don't understand how Maggie talked me into it. I mean, if this is love, you can keep it, it's too bloody dangerous. No, I'm not being wet. You don't know Mrs Crabs. She's horrible. She'll do *anything*.

Even her room gave me the creeps. It was disgusting. She had a pink quilted wardrobe ... I'm telling you! I'd heard the stories but I never believed it before now. Her dressing table was about as big as a grand piano. It looked like you should have played it, not done your face in it. Everything was pink and gold, even the carpet, except it had this horrible dark stain right next to the bed.

I thought ... what the fuck's that? Then I realised. It was blood. This must've been where they left Joey during Christmas dinner. They'd wrapped him up in plastic bags, but he must have leaked.

I mean, pervy, or what? I stared at that stain on the carpet and I nearly shat meself just thinking about it. The bed was enormous, you could have hid a football team in it. I had this horrible feeling it was alive, watching everything I did.

Of course, that wasn't where Eddie slept. He had a little two and a half footer in the box room next door, so he didn't disturb her beauty sleep.

"Get on with it!" hissed Jeff next door.

I wrenched the carpet up with me crowbar and got to work. I felt better on the job, which was a mistake. I'd got the furniture shoved to one side, and I was levering the floorboards up when ...

"All right, son, how you doing, OK?" said a familiar voice. I looked up and there she was ... Mrs Crabs. Who else?

Chapter 5

People don't understand about Mrs C.
They say, "She's just a little old lady." They
say, "She can't be any worse than the last
gang leader, Harry Dobson." He once poured
a bottle of brandy down a bloke's trousers
and then dropped a match in after. The
bloke was wearing *nylon* trousers. Then
there was the time he found his girlfriend
was being unfaithful. He nailed her hands
and feet to the floor and set his dogs on her.

Well, Harry was mean, but he wasn't as
bad as Mrs Crabs. People think he was, but
they don't know. She's worse than anyone.
And now she had her hands on me.

I got up hefting the crowbar in my hand and tried to look tough. She smiled at me like Frankenstein's aunt. I said, "Where's …" and then shut my mouth.

There was a second while she waited for me to finish. "Where's who, son?"

I said, "Nah, nothing."

Mrs Crabs was leaning against the door frame in a comfortable manner. She leaned round and yelled, "Greg! Nick? Anyone else?"

"No one, mam."

So Jeff had got away.

Mrs Crabs fixed her evil eyes on me. "Right, Mikey. You've got some explaining to do." She leaned forward and smiled at me. "Tell Auntie all about it."

I'm not brave, I know that. But being desperate helps. I turned, chucked the crowbar through the window and jumped out after it. OK, it was on the first floor and the window was double-glazed. But it was that or Mrs Crabs. I tell you … it was no contest.

The glass was still shattering as I went through it. I could feel it slicing up my arms. Then I was hurtling down in a hail of blood and glass. Down, down I went … it only took a second and then I crashed right into a bloody great rose bush under the sitting room window. I tried to get up but my ankles were broke. My first thought as the front door opened was that, yes, I had shat meself already.

Chapter 6

We had a little chat in the front garden, just for starters. Mrs Crabs suggested I was not the usual sort of shit she had on the roses, but as I was there already, her son Greg would be quite happy to chop me up and dig me in with the spade, if I liked.

I said, thanks, but I'd rather not. I put it to her that I was already fairly badly smashed about. Perhaps we could consider that side of things already dealt with? Then we could get straight on to the next stage of me begging them to stop and telling them everything I knew …

"That hardly seems right to me, son," said Mrs Crabs. "We have to do things in the right order now, don't we." She gave a nod to Nick and Greg, who lifted me gently by my arms and ankles and carried me indoors, swaying me slightly from side to side as they went.

****

I learned a lot over the next few days. You have to hand it to Mrs Crabs, she really knows her stuff. The thing that sets her apart from everyone else is her timing. It's all in the mind, see. I never really thought about that side of it before. Most people just grab hold of a bloke and do him over. The bloke doesn't like it and he tells you what you want to know to make you stop.

But that's nothing. That's just a battering. It's kid's stuff. I can see that now. It's timing that turns an ordinary battering into real torture.

It went on for ages and I tell you, even before they lay a finger on you, the torture never stops. There was old Eddie Crabs rubbing his little hands together, going, "Come on, Mrs Crabs, let's do him."

And she'd say, "No, no, no Eddie. You're going too fast. I don't think Mikey is ready for a session with Nick and Greg yet, are you Mikey? You need a bit more rest, son."

And I'd say, "It doesn't matter when you do it, Mrs Crabs. I've nothing to tell you." Then I'd get a little kick in the leg and be left there for a few hours to pee myself and crap myself and get hungry and thirsty before they came back for another little chat.

I swear no one barely touched me for the first day. Hardly at all. At first you think, great! A few more hours without torture.

But after a few hours, you really want them to get on with it ... you know, get it over with. And by the time you've been woken up for the seventh time that night, you can't fucking wait. Now, those stories about me begging her to set Nick and Greg on me, they aren't true. But I'll tell you, when they did I was bloody ready for it, that's all.

Worst thing about it was, she didn't believe me even when I told her. I held out for a little bit ... just to make it seem convincing really. They always feel they have to do something to you to get at the truth. But when I explained how we'd found out about her and Primo, she started laughing her little grey head off.

"Me, Primo's mother? You stupid sod, Mikey. I've never heard such a load of shite in all me life. Boys ..."

I only got her to believe my story in the end because she reckoned I was too thick to make it up myself.

42

Chapter 7

I spent the next few days bound hand and foot lying in a puddle of shit and piss in the Old Bag's cellar. There were frequent visitors, in the form of Greg and Nick and Mr and Mrs Crabs. They cleaned me up a couple of times, when she took me up to her bedroom to show me her dressing table. Nail clippers, nail files, hat pins, nail varnish remover and the like. It's amazing how much pain can be caused using these simple household items. I know. She showed me ... personally.

Next thing I know, I'm hanging upside down from the ceiling in the sitting room.

Mr Crabs was putting down not newspaper, but sheets to keep the carpet clean. They hadn't been letting me use the loo.

"It's all right, I've been," I kept telling them, which wasn't strictly true. Actually I was busting, but I was trying to hold it in because I was desperate not to meet the lads with wet trousers. But I'd held out longer than I thought I'd have to and now I was regretting it. Let's face it … it's better to have already pissed yourself before it all started than do it in front of everyone. Especially when you're hanging upside down.

All the local bosses had been called in to watch. They stood round me in a circle with their minders, holding handkerchiefs over their faces. There was Needles, the Creel brothers and about half a dozen others.

"Jesus, he stinks. Couldn't you have turned the hose on him?" said Needles.

"No one told me where the little boy's room is," I said, and Nick kicked me in the ear.

"Shut yer mouth you grassing little bastard," he snarled. Like I say, I was dying to go and I nearly wet meself. But I couldn't let that go.

"I never grassed no one ..."

"Shut up!" snapped Nick. He punched me in the stomach and that was it ... I couldn't hold it any longer. I pissed meself. Once I started I couldn't stop. It ran up me chest and over me face and round me ears and poured out of me hair onto the sheets. They all stared like I was a side-show.

"There better not be any of that getting through to my carpets or there'll be hell to pay," said Mrs Crabs. I twisted round to look at her. I was too scared to look her in the face, but I was very familiar with those pink fluffy slippers with the swollen ankles sticking out of them ... there they were, right by her stick.

I said, "It weren't my fault, Mrs Crabs. I had to stick by the family, I didn't know they was spinning me a line."

"Shut yer trap ..."

"But I never grassed no one ..."

"Shurrup!" She lifted her stick and aimed at me face and I shut up quick.

"He's been in with the Milligans the whole time," she said, and she gave me that horrible smile of hers, all false teeth and wrinkles. "Haven't you, Mikey?"

"I didn't know!"

"It doesn't matter what you know or don't know ... you don't grass folk up."

"But I never grassed ... ah!" Whack! Round came the stick. Mrs Crabs was breathing heavily. She doesn't like being told she's wrong.

"I think we might as well finish this off, gentlemen," she hissed. She lifted her stick again. I closed my eyes. Life wasn't all that fun at the minute, but even so, I tell you, I didn't want it to stop. You never want it to stop. Even the Old Bag couldn't make me want it to stop.

But Needles interrupted her. "Hang on a minute, Mrs Crabs. I need to ask you about this."

There was a pause. There was a rustle of paper. I twisted round desperately. Needles was holding out a piece of official looking paper. A birth certificate. Primo's birth certificate.

"Came through the post this morning. Easy enough to find out if it's forged or not, I should think."

The atmosphere changed very quickly. Greg and Nick backed off to the edges of the room. So did the bosses' minders. There was a nasty pause. Then there was some more rustling as the other bosses produced more pieces of paper out of their pockets. Greg and Nick glanced at Mrs Crabs ... and went for their guns. In the same second, so did everyone else. The room was filled with clicks as everyone cocked their weapons. Then, silence.

"Well, this is very odd," said Needles. "I wouldn't have expected this sort of reaction from a silly forgery like this."

Mrs Crabs was furious. "You get your boys to put their guns away, Needles. We can deal with this without shooters," she snapped. But no one moved.

"You first," said Needles. "Your boys started it. They can stop it, right lads?" Around the room, the other bosses nodded their heads.

From my place upside down in the middle of the room, I could see everything. The situation looked very deadly indeed. The minders were all around the edges of the room with their guns out. The Old Bag and the bosses were standing in the middle of the room, around me. There must have been about ten shooters pointing at them.

It was a stand off.

"You fucking idiots," hissed Mrs C, sounding like death on ice. "It's a set-up. They're forgeries."

"I daresay," said Needles, "but perhaps you better get your boys to put their guns away anyway, Mrs C."

But she didn't … she couldn't. It had gone too far already.

I'd had enough. "For God's sake, can't one of you bastards get me down?" I groaned. Very slowly, Dave Creel, bless him, put his hand in his pocket and took out a penknife. He sawed at the rope and down I came, face first, smack onto the carpet at Mrs Crabs' feet.

"Fuck," I moaned. But she had more to worry about than me.

"Gimme that here," she growled, and she snatched the certificate out of Needles' hand. She hung her stick over her arm and squinted down at the paper.

"It *is* a bloody forgery," she snapped. All the local bosses squinted at her. You could see what they were thinking. Why is she sounding surprised? Was it real? Was it a set-up? What was going on?

It was a very dangerous situation for all concerned. Various pieces of hardware were pointing at various heads and hearts. Fingers were itchy. Mrs Crabs' little eyes were swivelling about. Set-up or not, she was in trouble. No one had a clue what was going on.

"Perhaps the best thing to do would be for everyone to go home and we can sort this out later," suggested Needles.

"You're not going anywhere until I know who's behind this," snapped Mrs Crabs. But she wasn't getting her way this time. Needles was already edging towards the door when the answer to the problem came wailing up the road.

Police sirens.

"Ah ..." said Needles. He looked at Mrs Crabs. "Friends of yours?" he asked.

Normally everyone would have bolted for the door. But this time, with guns pointing at everyone's heads, there was no choice but to stand still. No one even dared put their weapons away. They just had to stand there and wait. Needles and the others looked sick. They thought Mrs Crabs' friends, the filth, had come to help her out.

Dave Creel pulled a face and spat suddenly at her foot. For a second everyone stared at the shiny little blob of gob on her pink fluffy slipper. I don't know how he dared. She's only about five foot tall but she looked like a fucking cobra. She suddenly lashed out at him with her stick, smack, right across his face. It was half an inch from a massacre. All the blokes around the edges shouted.

"OI!"

The figures in the middle of the room froze.

"Leave it," said Dave Creel, wiping the blood from his face. And ... there we stayed. The sirens were yelling outside now and no one dared so much as twitch. Even when the filth stopped knocking on the door and kicked it in, no one dared move an inch.

Four armed police came in ... quietly, no running, no shouting. It was as if they knew the situation called for a little caution.

And you know what? I knew one of them. It was Jeff, the black bloke with two holes in his nose where the rings usually went. It took a moment for me to recognise him in uniform, but it was him all right. He glanced at me out of the corner of his eye. I kept my mouth shut.

"Now boys, now boys. Guns down, boys," he said. "We don't want any trouble. We're just here to ask Mrs Crabs and her lads a few questions."

A little sigh went around the room. So … it was true. The police had come to rescue her. There's nothing worse for a reputation than getting rescued by the filth, know what I mean?

The bosses were glad enough to let them go, although Mrs Crabs and her lads didn't seem all that pleased about it.

"I've been set up," she hissed, and she even lashed out at one of the coppers. They took it in their stride. Jeff and another bloke took her carefully by the arm and led her forward. Just to polish it off, he leaned over her and said in a quiet voice … "We had a tip off, Mrs Crabs." Which helped seal the matter, so to speak.

After they'd all gone, everyone stood around shaking their heads.

"Who'd have thought it … in with the filth the whole time," said Needles. "How many blokes has she seen off for grassing? Twenty-odd?"

"It's been mass murder," said Dave Creel. For my part, I could have said more. Like for instance, the fact that the black guy was a pal of Maggie's. But I figured I'd done enough talking over the past few days to last me a lifetime. I kept my mouth shut.

Then there was a knock on the door and in comes Charlie and Brenda Milligan and Maggie. "Right boys," says Maggie. "Let's get down to business."

Chapter 8

And that was that. We never saw nothing of Mrs Crabs and her boys again. I don't know where the old filth hid them away. Spain, maybe. A lot of gangsters end up on the Costa del Sol, but no one's seen her there yet. If they do, she'll be paid a little visit. There's a lot of people in Manchester who would like to pay her back for all the lads she sold off to the filth over the years.

Primo's still about. People were a bit surprised about that. They thought he'd be off once his main supply of information dried up. Perhaps the police thought it would be a bit too obvious. No doubt he knows where his mam is hiding out. Maybe he wants to keep an eye on the rest of us to make sure we don't get near her.

Maggie's the top dog now. Would you believe it? Not Charlie, not Brenda – my Maggie! I keep remembering that time in the bookshop when she looked so helpless and I felt so sorry for her. How on earth did someone like her manage to beat the Old Bag herself? See, there's more to our Maggie than meets the eye …

And me? I'm at home, getting better every day. Maggie's even talking about us getting married. In bed with the boss, I am. A very good position to be in, you might think.

Only things aren't all that simple. They never bloody are, are they? There's a few things I know that the rest of the lads don't know. For starters, it's no wonder Mrs Crabs was so surprised that day. Those photos and papers were forged. Joey Milligan had been doing them at home on his PC for years. But don't get me wrong. That doesn't mean the whole thing was a set up. Maggie explained everything. The forgeries were just a back-up system, in case the Old Bag got rid of the real ones. And it was just as well, because when we did get the floor boards up in the Old Bag's house, there was nothing there.

"She must have already hidden them somewhere else," said Maggie. "Pity, but never mind. She's gone now, anyway."

We ripped the house to bits several times, but they never did turn up.

Of course, Needles and the Creel brothers and the others don't know that. No point in letting them in on that little secret ... they might get the wrong idea.

And you know what? They're not the only ones to be kept in the dark. I get the feeling there's more going on than the Milligan family tells me. For instance ... what about that bloke, Jeff? Needles and the rest of them don't know that he was working with Maggie. So ... was he a copper or wasn't he? If he was, then Maggie was working with the filth all along, just as the Old Bag claimed.

And if he wasn't a copper, then who was it that took Mrs Crabs and her boys away that day? If they were just a bunch of thugs that Maggie dressed up in uniform, then the Crabs won't be in Spain at all. It's no wonder no one's seen them. They'll be rotting away at the bottom of the Manchester ship canal, or lying in a hole up on the moors with a bullet in the back of their heads.

Well. No one's ever bothered explaining it all to me, and I haven't asked. There are some things it's better not to know. Know what I mean?

It seems to me I know a little too much and a little too little. Let's face it, I'm just piggy in the middle, aren't I? Maybe it's like Maggie said, and the Old Bag had a deal with Primo ... but maybe it's not. Maybe there never were any birth certificates and scrap books and photos, except the ones that Joey Milligan forged. In which case, me spending a week's holiday with Mrs Crabs and her lads was just another part of the plan. You know, make it look convincing, have them beat the shit out of Mikey for a week or two. Right?

And another thing, I don't like the way

things are going at home. Maggie's been on at me lately to do more housework. She reckons that as she's the main money earner, I ought to be helping out a bit more. She says housework would be good exercise for my legs. What's more, she's booted me out of the big bedroom and put me in the little two and a half footer in the spare room instead. She reckons me tossing and turning and moaning in pain all night keeps her awake.

Some of the lads have started to call me Eddie behind my back. Well, I'm not going to turn into another Eddie Crabs. No way.

So, I tell you ... I'm out of here. Soon as me legs get better.

Of course, I'll have to make sure Maggie's settled in first. I know she can be a bit of a nag about the housework, but the thing is, she needs me, see. That's why I don't mind

so much sleeping in the little bed. She's got
a lot on, she needs her sleep. That's what
the lads don't realise.

And she gets scared, too. Sometimes,
when I'm telling her that I need more respect,
she hangs her head and I know she's trying to
fight off the tears.

"You won't leave me, Mikey, will you?"
she whispers. "I don't think I can cope if you
leave me on my own."

Then she puts her arms around me and
holds me tight, and it feels like my heart's
going to break in half. She's only a little
thing, my Maggie. One day, when I'm sure
she's safely in charge, I'll clear off. She'll
come to visit me in my little bed and she'll
find out that Mikey ain't the one to turn into
Mummy's little helper. But until then, if she
needs someone to vacuum the carpet and
hold her when it all gets too much … I
suppose I'll just have to put up with it.

Meet the Author

I was born in Sussex, and spent my childhood dozing and dreaming the time away. I could not get down to work at all. I did badly at all exams but I didn't care. I'd decided ages before I wanted to write books.

When I left school, I was out of work, mainly, but I did building jobs on the side. I wrote things from time to time, but I wasn't really bothered. It was only when I was 35 that I thought I'd better get down to it, if I wanted to be a writer. My first book was called Cry of the Wolf. Since then, I've published 11 books. I'm now doing what I have always wanted – to write full-time. I think writing is the best job in the world.

I have a son, a daughter and a stepson. I live with my wife, Judith, in Manchester, in a Victorian house with lots of pets.

Hard-hitting short reads from Barrington Stoke

CRIME

Prisoner in Alcatraz	Theresa Breslin	1-84299-150-7 / 978-1-84299-150-3
Bloodline	Kevin Brooks	1-84299-202-3 / 978-1-84299-202-9
Twocking	Eric Brown	1-84299-042-X / 978-1-84299-042-1
Old Bag	Melvin Burgess	1-84299-422-0 / 978-1-84299-422-1
Partners in Crime	Nigel Hinton	1-84299-102-7 / 978-1-84299-102-2
Snapshot	Robert Swindells	1-84299-347-X / 978-1-84299-347-7

DRAMA

I See You Baby	Kevin Brooks & Catherine Forde	1-84299-330-5 / 978-184299-330-9
Baby Baby	Vivian French	1-84299-061-6 / 978-1-84299-061-2
Falling Awake	Vivian French	1-84299-438-7 / 978-1-84299-438-2
The Wedding Present	Adele Geras	1-84299-348-8 / 978-1-84299-348-4
No Stone Unturned	Brian Keaney	1-84299-349-6 / 978-1-84299-349-1
Stalker	Anthony Masters	1-84299-081-0 / 978-1-84299-081-0
The Blessed and the Damned	Sara Sheridan	1-84299-008-X / 978-1-84299-008-7

HORROR

Before Night Falls	Keith Gray	1-84299-124-8 / 978-1-84299-124-4
The Dogs	Mark Morris	1-902260-76-7 / 978-1-902260-76-1

SF

House of Lazarus	James Lovegrove	1-84299-125-6 / 978-1-84299-125-1